j 398.068 Thiaa

THIS FOR THAT
A Tonga Tale

retold by Verna Aardema
pictures by Victoria Chess

Dial Books for Young Readers  New York

This for That: A Tonga Tale
is a revision of a story by the same name
that appeared in *Behind the Back of the Mountain* by Verna Aardema,
published by The Dial Press, 1973, and now out of print.
The previous source is "Master Rabbit and the Berries" in *Specimens
of Bantu Folklore from Northern Rhodesia* by J. Torrend,
published by Kegan Paul, Trench, Trubner, London, 1921.

Published by Dial Books for Young Readers
A Division of Penguin USA Inc.
375 Hudson Street · New York, New York 10014

Library of Congress Cataloging in Publication Data
Aardema, Verna. This for that: a Tonga tale/
retold by Verna Aardema; pictures by Victoria Chess.
—1st ed. p. cm.
Summary: Rabbit tricks the other animals of the African
plain into giving her food and other treats.
ISBN 0-8037-1553-6 (trade). —ISBN 0-8037-1554-4 (lib. bdg.)
[1. Folklore, Tonga.] I. Chess, Victoria, ill. II. Title.
PZ8.1.A213Th 1997 398.24'529322—dc20 [E] 93-32309 CIP AC

*The artwork was rendered in watercolor and with Pelikan sepia,
which is no longer available in the United States.*

To my great-grandchild, Stephanie Aardema
V. A.

For Jennie DiMascio, with love
V.C.

In an arid region north of the Limpopo River there once was a water hole where animals came to drink. One morning when Rabbit went there, she found only dried mud.

A lion and then an elephant came. They began to dig a well. The sand flew, *chuh, chuh, chuh*.

The rabbit did not help at all. But when water finally came into the hole, she was the first to try to drink.

Lion growled, "Grrr! Go away, Rabbit. You did not help dig, so no water for you!"

Reluctantly Rabbit hopped away, *ka-pu-tu, ka-pu-tu*. Soon she met an ostrich. "Oh, Ostrich," she cried, "Lion and Elephant have a well and they won't let me drink."

"Come with me," said Ostrich. "I will find us some watery berries." With his sharp eyes he did find some. The two ate and ate. Then they picked the rest of the berries and hid them under a thornbush.

Later that day Rabbit went back to see if the berries were safe. They were. She ate one, then another, and another, *lup, lup, lup.* They tasted so good—she ate them all up!

At that moment she saw the ostrich coming. She did not have time to hide. So she called out, "Oh, Ostrich, someone ate our berries!"

Ostrich looked under the thornbush. The berries WERE gone. He said, "If I find the one who ate those berries, I'll kick him to the moon!"

Rabbit did not want to be kicked. So she said, "Ostrich, you ate them yourself. You are the only one who knew where they were."

"I did NOT!" cried Ostrich.

"Pay me for my berries," demanded Rabbit.

"Pay for berries I didn't eat? I won't!" said Ostrich.

"Pay me with a feather," said Rabbit. "Then one of us will be happy."

"Oh, well," said the ostrich, "if a feather will make you happy, here. . . ." And he gave the rabbit a beautiful plume from his tail.

Rabbit went off laughing softly to herself, *huh, huh, huh*. Soon she came upon a man who was cooking a chunk of meat over a fire.

When the man saw the ostrich plume the rabbit was carrying, he said, "Let me feel that feather." He took it and stroked it. Then he put it on his head and danced around the fire.

But the wind caught the plume and blew it into the fire.
TUUUUH! went the flames. And the feather was gone.
Rabbit sang:

> "Oh, my feather is gone,
>   The feather I got for my berries;
>   The berries that are all eaten up.
>   Oooh, now I have nothing."

"Don't be sad, Little Rabbit," said the man. "I'll give you
my meat instead."

Rabbit took the meat and went on her way. Presently she met
a woman who was carrying a bowl of sour milk on her head.

The woman said, "Will you give me that meat for this good
sour milk?"

"No," said Rabbit. "But you make a fire and heat the meat, and I will let you eat it with me. I will sleep under this tree. And you must call me when the meat is ready." Then she lay down and slept.

But when the meat was hot, the woman did not call the rabbit. She ate it herself, as fast as she could, *yatua, yatua, yatua.*

When the rabbit woke up, there was nothing left but the bone. She sang:

"Oh, my meat is gone,
   The meat I got for my feather;
   The feather I got for my berries;
   The berries that are all eaten up.
   Oooh, now I have nothing."

"Here," said the woman, "take this sour milk instead."

Rabbit took the sour milk and went on her way. But she did not want the sour milk, and she pondered about how to get rid of it.

Farther on Rabbit came to a large anthill. "I know," she said. "The ants will pay for my sour milk." Up the anthill she scrambled with the bowl of milk. Near the top she slipped. The milk slopped out! And Rabbit and the bowl went rolling down, *denkyi, denkyi, du.*

Soon the Ant Queen came out. And Rabbit said to her, "See
what your hill did!" Then she sang:

> "Oh, my sour milk is gone,
>   The milk I got for my meat;
>   The meat I got for my feather;
>   The feather I got for my berries;
>   The berries that are all eaten up.
>   Oooh, now I have nothing."

The Ant Queen said to her workers, "Fill her bowl with winged ants." And they did.

Rabbit set off with the bowl of winged ants. "Lion will like these," she said. "Now I will go to the well and get water." She hurried back to the well and found the lion still guarding it.

"Look, Lion," said Rabbit. "See what I have? Winged ants! I'll give them to you in exchange for some water."

"Go away!" snarled the lion. "Elephant would be mad at me if I let you have water."

"I know how to trick Elephant," said Rabbit. "You pretend to sleep, and I'll tie you up. Then you can say that you could not stop me."

Now, Lion did like winged ants. But he did not like to catch them one by one. He looked at the bowl full of them, and said, "Tie me up, Rabbit."

Rabbit found a long vine, and she wound it around the tree and the lion, *b-long, b-long, b-long.* As she worked, the lion asked, "Where did you get all those winged ants?"

Rabbit said, "Ant Queen gave them to me for my sour milk."

"What sour milk?" asked Lion.

"The milk I got for my meat."

"What meat?"

"The meat I got for my feather."

"What feather?"

"The feather I got from Ostrich for the berries he did not eat."

"WHAT?" cried Lion.

"I ate them and told him HE did," laughed Rabbit.

At that moment, out of the bush came Ostrich. His wings were spread, so he looked three times his size. "HUNN!" he roared. "So it was YOU who ate the berries!"

"Don't kick me! Don't kick me!" begged the rabbit. "I'll pay you for the berries. I'll pay you with these good winged ants."

"You can't pay him with MY ants," cried Lion.

"But I didn't give them to you yet," said Rabbit.

"Give them to me NOW!" bellowed the lion.

But Rabbit gave the ants to Ostrich. Then she ran to the well to get a drink. Just as she began to lap the water, Lion roared, "WOOOOAH!"

Rabbit was so scared, she fell *lopp* into the water. "Help!" she cried.

Ostrich reached in and plucked her out. Then he sat down and let the rabbit climb onto his back with the bowl of winged ants in her arms.

Just then, out of the bush came Elephant.

"Oh, Elephant," cried Lion, "get me away from this tree. I have to catch that rabbit."

Elephant said, "I don't know how to get a lion away from a tree. But I know how to get a tree away from a lion." She wrapped her trunk around the tree, and GBAT! Up it came! But the lion was still tied to it.

Ostrich set off, *tuk-pik, tuk-pik, tuk-pik*, with Rabbit holding the bowl of ants and clinging to his back.

After them came the elephant carrying the tree with the roaring, kicking lion still tied to it. Soon the ostrich and the rabbit were far ahead.

Rabbit was so happy! She said, "Oh, Ostrich, I love you!" And she snuggled against the big bird's skinny neck. But as she did, she dropped the bowl, and away went the ants—all over the path!

"Wolu!" wailed Rabbit. For now she had nothing to give to Ostrich to pay him for the berries and to make up for the lie she had told.

And when the bowl of winged ants fell, Ostrich shook her off his back. Then he kicked her so hard that—though she did not go as high as the moon—she saw stars.

Lion and Elephant saw this, and they were pleased that justice had been done. . . .

And when Ostrich helped untangle Lion from the tree, he said, "A lie may travel far, but the truth will overtake it."